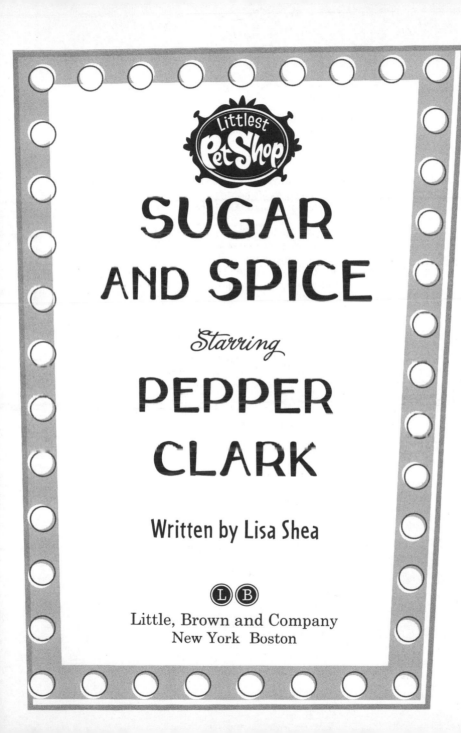

Littlest Pet Shop

SUGAR
AND SPICE

Starring

PEPPER
CLARK

Written by Lisa Shea

Ⓛ Ⓑ

Little, Brown and Company
New York Boston

Little, Brown and Company

Hachette Book Group
1290 Avenue of the Americas, New York, NY 10104
Visit us at lb-kids.com

Little, Brown and Company is a division of Hachette Book Group, Inc. The Little, Brown name and logo are trademarks of Hachette Book Group, Inc.

The publisher is not responsible for websites (or their content) that are not owned by the publisher.

First Edition: September 2016

Library of Congress Control Number: 2016943525

ISBN 978-0-316-39523-6

10 9 8 7 6 5 4 3 2 1

RRD-C

Printed in the United States of America

For Ann and Leslie.

CONTENTS

Chapter 1

"*Mmmm!* Fresh coffee!" Pepper said, sniffing happily as the aroma of French roast filled the air. She curled around Blythe's legs like a happy kitten.

"Blythe, I do believe that skunk likes the smell of coffee!" Mrs. Twombly said with a laugh.

"Oh, I don't think it's that, Mrs. Twombly,"

Blythe replied. "I think Pepper's just happy because sometimes when I make a fresh pot of coffee, I give her a little treat." Blythe knelt down and offered Pepper a few crumbs of a glazed doughnut, which Pepper ate daintily out of her hand.

"*Mmmm!* I do love glazed doughnuts," Pepper said to Blythe. "But I love the smell of fresh coffee, too! Just because I'm a skunk, people think I can't appreciate things that smell nice, but I do!" Blythe gave a little laugh and stroked Pepper's shiny fur. Blythe had a special gift. She understood every word Pepper said, but of course nobody else could. Instead of just hearing the pets squawk and squeal and bark and purr, she actually heard words when the animals spoke. But this special talent was top secret. Nobody knew Blythe could communicate with animals, not even her boss, Mrs. Twombly.

"Blythe, it never ceases to amaze me how these pets seem to try to talk to you," Mrs. Twombly said. "Like just now, I could swear Pepper was speaking directly to you!"

"Oh, Pepper and I are old friends," Blythe replied. "We know each other pretty well."

"Well, don't give her too many treats—or any of the other pets, either," Mrs. Twombly warned. "We're going to need every single treat for the big 'buy one, get one free' day to promote the Pawrista's Café next weekend. I expect a huge crowd—and hopefully they will all be hungry—and thirsty!"

"I'm looking forward to it," Blythe said. "I think it's going to be a lot of fun."

"I'm so glad you said that," Mrs. Twombly said. "Because I've been thinking. I would like to give you a bit more responsibility. I'm putting you in charge of this event. Oh, don't worry—of course I'll be around to help out. But I would like for you to really be in charge. You decide what coffees to serve, what treats to make, how to decorate the café, etcetera, etcetera. What do you think?"

Blythe hesitated for a moment. It sounded like a lot of work. But Pepper whispered, "Do it, Blythe! And you know we'll all help you!"

"Thank you, Mrs. Twombly, I'd love to be in charge," Blythe said. She smiled. "And I'm sure all the pets will help me."

Mrs. Twombly laughed. "Help you? I'm sure you'll have to watch them extra carefully around all the yummy treats you'll be serving. But I'm glad you said yes. Thank you!" And Mrs. Twombly walked away, singing a happy tune.

Pepper turns to Blythe. "I'm glad you said yes, too, Blythe!" she said. "And everyone *will* help out—just you wait and see!"

Blythe looked doubtful. "I really don't know much about running a business, or about coffee for that matter," she said. "But I didn't want to let Mrs. Twombly down."

By now, a few more of the pets had gathered around Blythe and Pepper.

"Don't worry, Blythe, you'll be great!" Penny Ling, a sweet and graceful panda said.

"And you know that I'll help you any way I can," Russell told her. Russell was a hedgehog, and the most practical member of the group.

"And you know with me in your corner, it will be the most fabulous coffee shop event ever!" Zoe cheered. Everyone agreed. There was no one more glamorous than Zoe, a Cavalier King Charles spaniel who was fond of saying "Style" was her middle name.

"Sunil and I will be at your beck and call," Vinnie, a dancing gecko, promised. "We'll all make sure your event is a huge hit."

"Thanks, guys," Blythe said. "I do feel a little more relieved now."

"Let's celebrate!" Pepper insisted. "How about a little more glazed doughnut for your old pal Pepper?"

"Just a couple of crumbs," Blythe said, handing them over. "Remember, a little sugar goes a long way."

Pepper silently disagreed. *If a little sugar*

makes me feel good, then a lot of sugar would make me feel great*!* she thought to herself. *Blythe just worries too much.* And when she wasn't looking, Pepper grabbed a few more crumbs from the doughnut box to save for later. She just *loooooved* sweets!

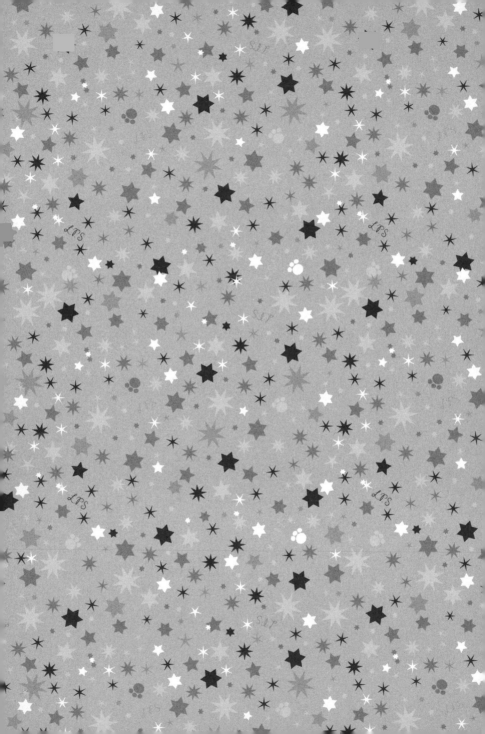

Chapter 2

"*Bonjour, mes amis,*" Zoe sang out to her friends the next morning.

"Huh?" Vinnie asked, looking confused.

"It's French," Zoe explained. "And it's going to be the perfect theme for the Pawrista's party. French! Everything French! French berets! French roast coffee! French food..."

"French fries?" Vinnie said hopefully.

Zoe laughed. "Well, not French fries, but French pastries and croissants."

"Even better," Vinnie said. "Sounds good to me, Zoe!"

"I love it, too," Pepper chimed in. "Maybe I'll add some French jokes to my comedy act."

"Comedy act?" Sunil said, surprised. "Blythe didn't mention anything to us about that."

"Oh, I haven't gotten a chance to discuss it with her yet," Pepper said. "But I'm sure Blythe will say yes. Why wouldn't she?"

"Why wouldn't I say yes to what?" Blythe asked, suddenly appearing from around the corner.

"My comedy routine," Pepper said proudly. "I'm working on a great act for the Pawrista's event."

Blythe hesitated. How could she explain to Pepper that most humans would run for the hills if asked to be in the same room as a skunk? Not to mention the fact that they wouldn't be able to understand her jokes, because only Blythe could communicate with the pets.

But when she looked at Pepper's shining face, she just couldn't refuse her—at least not completely. She stroked Pepper's fur and said, "Let me think about it, okay?"

Pepper nodded happily. She was sure Blythe would come around.

"And Zoe wants the café to have a French theme," Russell said.

"Yes, Blythe," Zoe said. "Just think of it—beautiful, fabulous France, right here in our pet shop!"

Blythe thought for a minute. "You know,

I hadn't really thought about a theme for the event, but that's not a bad idea," she said. "After all, who doesn't love Paris?"

"*Oui, oui!*" Zoe cried.

"Wee wee?" Pepper joked. "The restrooms are in the back, *madame*, Ha! Hey, that's pretty good. Maybe I'll use it in my act." She trotted off in search of a sweet treat and didn't see the worried look Blythe gave her as she left.

Sunil and Vinnie were all for a French theme—especially when Zoe said they could wear French berets and striped shirts. "I was born to wear a beret!" Sunil, a magic-loving mongoose said, studying his face in a mirror.

"We should learn a few key phrases in French," Vinnie added. "It will add to the theme of the day. Plus, who knows? Maybe we'll charm a few female pets. How do you say 'beautiful' in French, Zoe?"

"*Belle,*" Zoe responded.

"And how would you say, 'You are pretty'?"

"*Vous êtes jolie,*" Zoe told him.

"So '*belle*' is beautiful and '*jolie*' is pretty?" Sunil said.

"*Oui*—that means yes!" Zoe said with a laugh.

"It's like those French have a different word for everything!" Vinnie exclaimed.

Pepper laughed. "Hey, that's funny! You mind if I steal that for my act?" she asked.

Sunil and Vinnie exchanged a look.

"You know, Blythe didn't say you definitely were going to do a comedy routine," Sunil said. "She just said, 'Let me think about it.'"

"Which is just as good as saying yes!" Pepper replied. "Who wouldn't want free entertainment for their event? Hey, I just thought of another one: Why did the baker stop making doughnuts? Because he was bored with the hole business. Get it? *Hole? Whole? Hahaha!* I have a million of these! I need to start writing these down! But first, another little sweet treat before I go." Pepper rushed off in search of a snack.

Russell, meanwhile, was watching the entire exchange worriedly. "If Pepper doesn't get to do her comedy routine, it will break her heart," he thought out loud. "I should discuss this with Blythe before it really gets out of hand."

Just at that moment, Pepper returned, snacking on a broken piece of cupcake. "Hey, Russell, how does this sound?" she said. "The customer asks, 'Hey, waiter, are there cupcakes on the menu today?' 'No, I cleaned it off!' *Hahaha!*"

Russell managed a weak smile. *I really need to speak to Blythe about Pepper,* he thought.

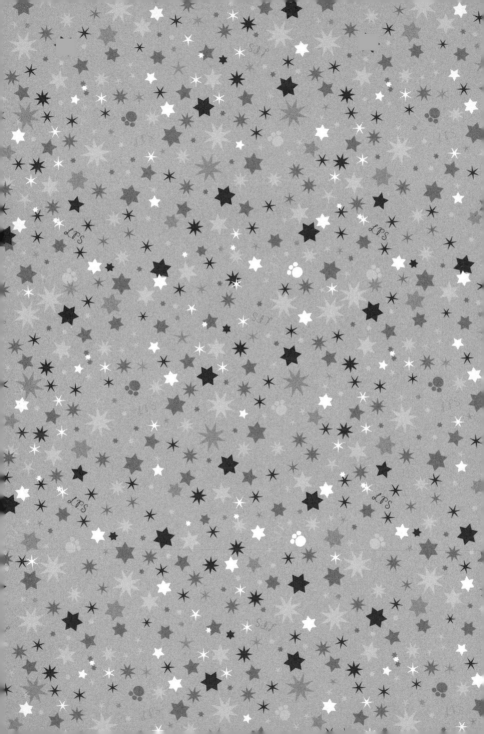

Chapter 3

Sunil and Vinnie were having a great time practicing their French, although they still had a lot to learn.

"I'm going to impress everyone with my French at the event," Vinnie said.

"Remember, it takes a while to learn a new language," Sunil told him. "I'll be more than happy just to be able to say a few phrases well."

"Not me," Vinnie said. "By the day of the event, I want to be able to hold an entire conversation in French and sound just like a Frenchman. I know I can do it if I practice long enough! I just need to keep speaking the language every day, as often as I can."

"Bon chance," Sunil said. "And, by the way, that means good luck."

Vinnie walked over to Zoe, his beret tilted at what he hoped was a striking angle. *"Bonjour, Zoe!"* he said brightly. *"Vous avez de beaux cheval!"* Then he gave Zoe a big wink.

Zoe looked startled. "What did you just say?"

"I *said*—or what I *wanted* to say was: 'You have beautiful hair,' " Vinnie said.

At this, Zoe began laughing hysterically.

"What? What did I say?" Vinnie asked worriedly.

"Well, you were close, I'll give you that," Zoe said. "You meant to say "*Cheveux*, not *cheval*. Instead of telling me I had beautiful hair, you actually were closer to calling me a beautiful horse."

Sunil couldn't stop laughing! "Smooth, Vinnie, real smooth," he said. "I'm sure everyone will be very impressed with your accent when you tell them what beautiful horses they are!"

Vinnie was totally unperturbed. "Don't you worry," he told Sunil. "The day of the event, I'll be ready. *Cheveux, cheveux, cheveux*," he repeated as he walked away.

Penny Ling, Pepper, and Minka, an artistic monkey, rushed over to Zoe. "Zoe, look! We love our Paris dresses!" Penny Ling said happily. All three were wearing black berets and black dresses with a white Eiffel Tower sketched on them. They all struck a pose.

"Oh, I'm so glad!" Zoe said. "I gave the idea to Blythe for your outfits. I told her you would like them. Simple, classy, elegant. Beautiful!"

"*Très jolie!*" Sunil agreed, and Minka and Penny Ling giggled.

"Hey, where's your dress, Zoe?" Pepper asked.

"Oh…mine is just a little bit different," Zoe said hesitantly. "So Blythe has to make a couple of alterations."

"What's different?" Minka asked. "Is your beret a different color or something?"

Zoe flushed. "Well…it's a little bit more than that…"

Now Pepper got a little suspicious. "Exactly how much more different, *cherie*?" she said.

Now Zoe was visibly nervous. "Just a little bit different. It's not black...and it doesn't have an Eiffel Tower...and I'm not wearing a beret...and...and..."

"Just say it," Pepper said impatiently.

Zoe sighed. "It'll be easier just to show you. I'll be right back," she said.

When she reappeared a few minutes later, everyone gasped. Instead of a beret she was wearing a feathered and sparkly headpiece, and instead of a plain black dress she was wearing a multicolored floral dress festooned with sequins, with at least three petticoats underneath.

"'A little bit different'?" Pepper snorted. "That's like saying chocolate ice cream is a little bit different than brussels sprouts!"

But Penny Ling and Minka were surprisingly unfazed. "It's beautiful, but we still like our dresses," Minka said. "And honestly, Pepper, would you want to wear that?"

"Not really," Pepper admitted. "It was just a bit of a shock."

"You guys know I like to be a little more fashion-forward than you do," Zoe said. "So I suggested my costume be like a French cancan girl. I didn't think you'd mind."

"It's fine," Pepper said.

"Really?" Zoe asked. "You're really okay with me wearing this?"

"No worries, Zoe," Pepper assured her. "You can-can wear-wear that outfit, with my blessing," she joked.

"Aw, thanks, Pepper." Zoe said. "I'm so glad! I'm really excited about this costume." She gave a little wiggle and her entire dress sparkled and shimmered just as Vinnie came back into the room. He looked at Zoe's glittery outfit and smiled.

"Wow! *Tu es très belle, ma petite pomme de terre!*" Vinnie exclaimed.

"Oh, Vinnie." Zoe sighed. "You just called me a beautiful little potato."

Vinnie shrugged. "Pardon *moi, mademoiselle,*" he said. "I guess it's back to the French book for me."

"And back to the kitchen for me," Pepper said. "Is anyone else hungry? I could go for a cupcake right about now…"

"Didn't I just see you eating a bit of lemon cake a little while ago?" Minka asked.

"Yes, what of it?" Pepper said. "So I'm hungry again. Writing funny jokes makes me hungry. I need a little cupcake…with a lot of icing! I'll be right back. I need to see if I can get Blythe or Mrs. Twombly to give me a little."

As she pranced off, Penny Ling looked at Minka. She was a little troubled.

"Has Pepper been eating more sweets lately?" she asked. "I'm a little worried about her. It's not healthy."

Minka shrugged. "I know she's been busy writing her comedy routine," she said. "So maybe she is a little stressed and eating a bit more. That's normal. Nothing to worry about."

Just then, Pepper reappeared. "I just thought of another joke!" she yelled.

"Why are you yelling?" Sunil asked.

"OH AM I YELLING?" Pepper yelled. "*SORRY!!!* Okay, here's the joke: A customer says, 'Waiter, this cake tastes funny.' And the waiter says, 'Then why aren't you laughing?'

BWHAHAHA! Isn't that a good one? Wait—so why aren't any of *you* laughing?" Pepper asked.

None of the pets were laughing. They were all staring at Pepper's glassy eyes, shrill voice, and hyper manner. What was going on with Pepper?

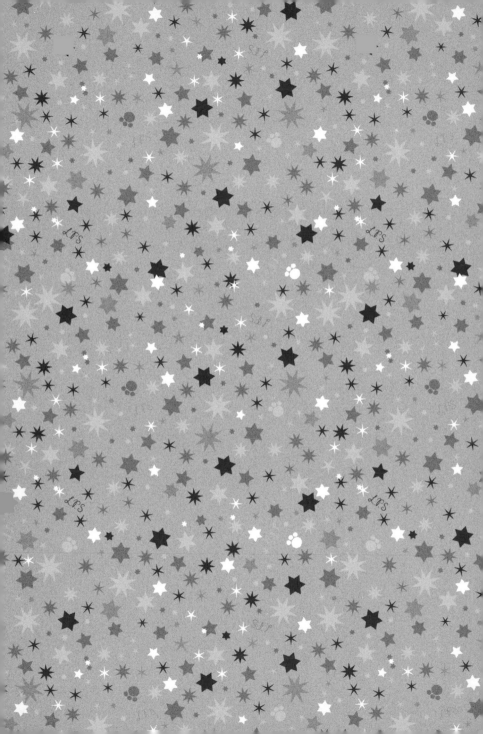

Chapter 4

Russell went looking for Blythe and found her sitting at a table with a notepad and a calculator, going over a list of numbers. She looked worried.

"What's going on, Blythe?" Russell asked.

Blythe showed Russell her notepad. "I really hope this event turns out to be a success," she said. "I spent more money than I planned on, but I really loved the idea of a French theme. So I went a little overboard on the costumes and decorations."

Russell looked at Blythe's notes and studied the list of figures. "Can you bake?" he asked. "You can save a lot of money if you bake some of the pastries yourself instead of ordering them in."

"*Hmmm,* that's not a bad idea," Blythe said. "And I love to bake! Maybe I'll make the cupcakes instead of ordering them. And we could look up ways to decorate the cupcakes online." Blythe was busy redoing her price list when she heard a voice.

"Hello, Blythe."

Blythe looked up and was shocked to see the Biskit twins, Brittany and Whittany, standing in front of her. As usual, they were dressed in the latest fashion, and their hair and nails were perfect. Despite all this, they both looked extremely uncomfortable.

"Brittany, Whittany! What are you two doing here?" Blythe asked. The girls exchanged nervous glances.

Brittany sighed. "Well, believe it or not, we're looking for work."

Blythe gasped. She couldn't help it. "Work? Why? You guys couldn't possibly need any money."

"We don't," Whittany said. "But our father said he's tired of seeing us just sitting around the house watching videos and reading fashion magazines."

"Daddy just doesn't understand that we're doing serious research. We're planning on being huge Internet stars," Brittany explains. "We're just studying the competition. Anyway, he said he'd cut off our allowance if we didn't get out of the house and find jobs." She paused. "So here we are."

Blythe was stunned. "You want to work here—for *me*?"

"Why not?" Whittany said. "I think it will be fun. And we're really good workers."

At this point, Russell tried to cover a laugh with a cough. It came out as a weird choking sound.

"Um, Blythe? I think your little porcupine here is choking," Brittany said.

Blythe couldn't suppress a smile. "He's a hedgehog, and I think he just found something a little hard to swallow." She gently patted Russell on the back. "Everything okay, buddy?" she asked. Russell smiled weakly.

Blythe looked back at the Biskit twins, who were staring at her blankly.

"Well, there aren't any openings here right now," Blythe said. "And even if there were, I don't think you would want to work here. I couldn't pay you very much."

"Oh, we could work for free," Brittany told her. "We'd be...what was that word Daddy used, Whittany? We'd be *volunteers*."

"Oh! Well, that's a little different," Blythe said. "But again, there aren't any openings right now, even for volunteers. I will definitely keep you in mind."

"Okay. Thanks, Blythe," Brittany said. "Come on, Whittany. Let's go home. I'm tired."

"Me, too," Whittany sighed. "This looking-for-work stuff is exhausting. Who knew?"

"Totally," Brittany agreed. "Although I wouldn't mind shopping for a new pair of boots first."

"*Oooh*, new boots," Whittany said. "And maybe a new bag to match? I feel my energy coming back already. Let's go, Brit. See ya, Blythe."

As they left the shop, Blythe gave Russell a stunned look.

"Imagine, Brittany and Whittany Biskit asking *me* for work!" she said. "They said they'd work for free. At least their price is right. Maybe I will take them up on that offer sometime."

At this, Russell starting laughing and coughing again.

"Oh, come on, it's not that funny," Blythe said.

"Yes it *is*!" Russell wheezed.

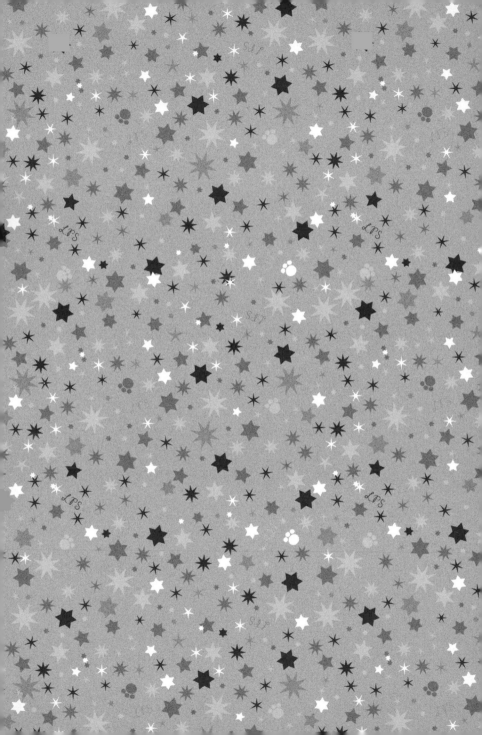

Chapter 5

It seemed like the Pawrista "buy one get one free" event was going to be a huge hit. People were talking about it on social media, and as the day of the event drew closer, the name Pawrista was trending. The phone was ringing off the hook with people asking questions about the pets and the event. "Are all the pastries two for one?" "And what kind of pets do you have?" "Can I take a selfie with each of them?"

Meanwhile, Pepper couldn't contain her excitement. She kept practicing her comedy routine. It was going to be a fantastic day. "People are going to remember the name Pepper Clark," she said as she looked into the mirror. Then she went out in search of the other pets to chat with, and also maybe to get some more coffee cake crumbs from Blythe.

A few customers were in the shop talking to Blythe about the event. "This is such a cute place," one woman said to Blythe. "I'm really looking forward to your special—*Gaaaah!*"

Her voice made both Blythe and Pepper jump. Pepper was curling herself around Blythe's legs, the way she always did when she wanted a snack.

"Is…that…a…a…*skunk*?" the woman shrieked.

Blythe rushed to Pepper's defense.

"It is, but you needn't worry, she never sprays, she actually is a very domesticated skunk. Her name is Pepper and…"

The woman gasped and threw some money on the counter and grabbed her doughnut.

"I'm sorry, but I absolutely cannot be in the same room as a skunk," she said. "And surely there must be some health-code violation about this. How can you possibly have a skunk around customers? And you can forget about me coming to your event! I wouldn't come back here if you were giving away pastries absolutely free!"

"Miss! Please come back!" Blythe begged. "I can assure you, Pepper will be nowhere near any customers the day of our event. I-I-I'll lock her up in a back room. You won't have to worry about her!"

"What did you just say?" Pepper said. Even the other pets gasped. "You'll lock me up in a back room? Did I hear that correctly?"

"Oh, Pepper, you know I didn't mean it like that," Blythe said. "But this event is just so important to me. I panicked. I'm so sorry. I can't take a chance on losing customers."

"I'm sorry, too," Pepper told her. "I know most people don't like skunks, so I always brace myself for a possible insult around strangers. But I never in my wildest dreams ever expected the worst insult of all would come from *you*."

"Pepper, please, wait!" Blythe begged.

But it was too late. Pepper rushed out of the room in tears. Blythe felt terrible.

Zoe sniffed the air. "What's that smell?" she asked Penny Ling.

"It's Pepper," Penny Ling said quietly. "And it smells like . . . sadness."

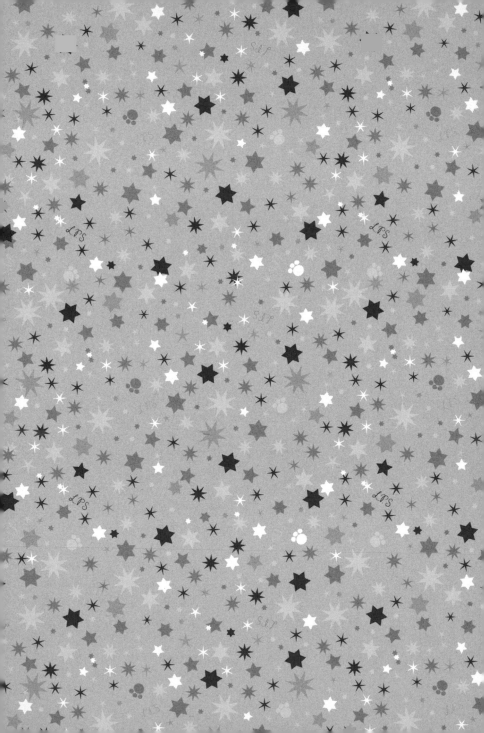

Chapter 6

Pepper stayed in bed the next day, refusing to talk to anyone. When Zoe, Minka, and Penny Ling tried to talk to her, she said, "Go away. Apparently I'm too hideous to talk to anybody. I'm just going to stay locked up back here, so nobody has to be offended by my smell, my voice, or my face."

The trio of pets quietly left Pepper's room.

They caught up with Russell, Sunil, and Vinnie to discuss the dilemma.

"This is bad," Zoe said. "I've never seen Pepper so upset. She doesn't want to see or talk to any of us."

"I just want to give her a big hug!" Penny Ling cried. "We need to think of something to cheer her up."

"But what can we do?" Zoe said. "She won't even leave her bed."

"What does Pepper love more than anything?" Minka asked. "What would make her feel happy again?"

Sunil and Vinnie looked at each other for a moment. Then they answered at the same time. "Performing!" they both said.

"Are you thinking what I'm thinking?" Sunil asked Vinnie.

"I am," Vinnie said. "It will take a little

work, but it can be done. And it will be worth it to see Pepper happy again."

Now that the pets knew just what to do to cheer Pepper up, they worked together as a team quickly. Russell helped them gather together a few props, and in a little while they had assembled a makeshift stage. Now they just had to coax Pepper out of her bed.

"Pepper, would you come with me, please?" Russell said politely.

Pepper looked up. Her eyes were red and puffy from crying.

"Russell, I know you mean well, but I'm just not in the mood for socializing," Pepper told him.

"This is more than socializing. Please don't say no, Pepper. You don't even know what this is about," Russell said. "Trust me, you won't be sorry."

"Why? What's going on? Is it some sort of party?"

"Sort of," Russell says.

"And I'm allowed to go? Are you sure Blythe wouldn't prefer I stay locked up in a closet somewhere?" Pepper asked bitterly.

"Pepper, you know Blythe really didn't mean that," Russell said earnestly. "And yes, of course you're allowed to come. As a matter of fact, this is a surprise we made especially for you. Now, close your eyes. Don't open them until I tell you it's okay."

Russell led Pepper to a corner of the pet shop, where the pets had set up a couple of planks of wood for a stage, and Zoe found a large flashlight to use as a spotlight. All the pets were gathered around in a semicircle, as Pepper's audience.

"Okay, you can open your eyes," he said.

Pepper opened her eyes and blinked—
the flashlight was shining right in her face!

"W-what's going on?" she stammered.

"Ladies and gentlemen, please allow
me to introduce the funniest pet ever,"
Sunil said. "Everybody put your hands—or
paws—together and give it up for the one,
the only...Pepper Clark!"

All the pets cheered.

Pepper was stunned. She turned to look
at Russell.

"Is this for real?" she said.

"It is," Russell assured her.

"Okay...so now what?" Pepper asked.

"Now..." Russell joined the other pets
on the floor. "You entertain us! Tell us some
jokes!"

Pepper was shocked but also thrilled.
"Really?"

"Really!" they shouted.

"Please, tell me a joke, Pepper!" Zoe shouted.

"Yeah, make me laugh!" Vinnie said.

"Well, okay then!" Pepper said. She looked around the room. "Let's get this show started. Let's see...Penny Ling, my friend. What's black and white and red all over? A panda with a sunburn!"

Penny Ling giggled and wiped her eyes. "*Ooh*, Pepper, I'm laughing so hard I'm crying!" Penny Ling said. Pepper grinned and continued with her routine.

"Zoe, this joke is for you. What dog loves to take bubble baths? A shampoodle!" *All* the pets laughed at that joke! "Minka! Why do monkeys love bananas? They are very a-*peel*-ing!" Minka squealed with delight at that one.

"Pepper, you're a natural comedienne. You always tell the best jokes!" Minka cried.

"Tell me something I don't know!" Pepper laughed. "Russell! What is a baby hedgehog after it's six days old? Seven days old! Vinnie! What kind of gecko can jump higher than a house? Any kind—a house can't jump!"

The pets laughed and laughed. They didn't realize that Blythe was standing behind a corner listening to everything that was going on. Suddenly, Blythe came out from behind the corner. She was applauding. The pets turned to look at her, and everything got very quiet. What was Blythe going to say to Pepper? Blythe walked over to Pepper and knelt down beside her. She looked deep into Pepper's eyes.

"Pepper, no one—and I mean no one,

pets or people—can tell a joke like you," Blythe said. "I was crazy to ever think you shouldn't be around for the Pawrista event. Would you please join us? And perform your comedy routine?"

"Why, Blythe, I thought you'd never ask!" Pepper said with a laugh. Blythe and Pepper hugged as all the pets cheered.

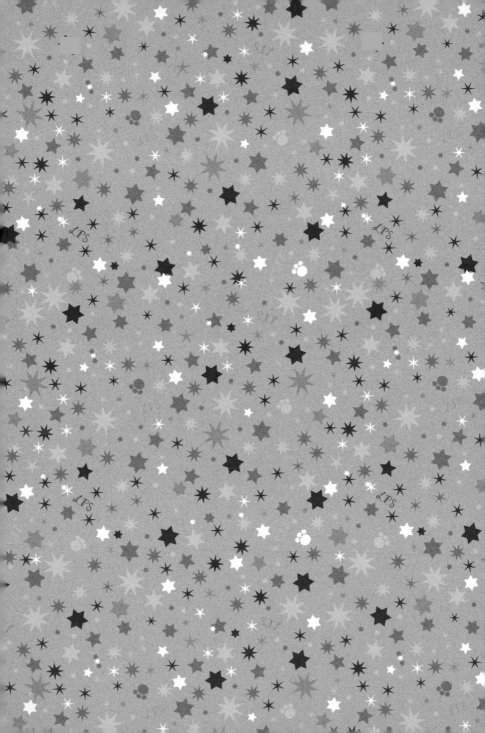

Chapter 7

The next morning did not start well at all. "Uh-oh," Russell said. He was staring at an open newspaper on the table. "This is definitely not going to make Blythe happy."

"What's the matter?" Sunil said. "Blythe and Pepper are friends again, and the preparations for the event are going smoothly. What's wrong?"

"This." Russell pointed to a page in the local newspaper. All the pets gathered around. Pepper read out loud.

"Come to Dollar Day at Kat's Coffee House," she read. "Everything will be on sale for one dollar only—any size coffee, tea, or hot cocoa! All pastries and cookies, too!"

"And look at the date," Russell said glumly.

"Oh no! It's the same day as our event!" Penny Ling cried. "That will ruin everything!"

"How can they do that?" Vinnie said angrily. "Blythe has been working so hard."

"It's not personal; it's just business," Zoe said. "It's not nice, but it's smart. If they don't do something to compete with our event, people who usually go to Kat's café for coffee or doughnuts might start coming here instead. They're not trying to hurt

Blythe, they're just trying to hang on to their customers. Kat's not being mean on purpose. It's just the way of the world."

"We just have to think of a way to make our event better than their dollar deals," Russell said thoughtfully.

The pets were all silently thinking when Blythe walked in.

"Good morning, all!" Blythe said cheerfully. She looked around the pet shop, and a room full of sad eyes looked back at her. "Uh-oh, what's wrong?" she asked. "Vinnie, Sunil, you guys have a fight?"

"No, we're fine, Blythe," Sunil said.

"Zoe, is there something wrong? Is your costume okay? Oh, wait—not enough sparkles for you?"

"Oh no, Blythe, my costume is perfect. It's gorgeous," Zoe replied.

"Then, geez, what's with all the sad eyes and faces? Somebody please say something. You guys are weirding me out," Blythe said.

Russell held up the newspaper and silently pointed.

Blythe read the blurb. She gulped. She tried to remain calm.

"Oh! Well…nothing like a little healthy competition," she said with a laugh. "It's fine, really. It doesn't matter. No worries." She forced herself to put on a brave smile. But the pets could tell she was concerned.

"Don't worry, Blythe, we'll think of something. We know how much this event means to you," Vinnie said.

"There's got to be a way to make our event better," Zoe said.

"I agree," said Pepper. "But how?"

"We need to think of something that we

have that Kat's Coffee House doesn't," Russell said. The pets all looked around the pet shop thoughtfully.

"I've got it!" Pepper yelled.

"Pepper, please," Penny Ling begged, covering her ears. "You really don't have to scream."

"Sorry, I'm just so excited," Pepper said.

"So what is it?" Sunil asked. "What have we got that Kat's Coffee House doesn't?"

"Us!" Pepper said proudly.

"What do you mean 'us'?" Zoe asked. "What do we have to do with selling coffee and pastries?"

"I read this article about a new craze in cafés, where people pay to play with puppies and kittens after they've had their snack and a beverage," Pepper explains.

"You mean you want us to play with the

customers?" Vinnie asked. "I don't know about that…"

"No, we don't have to play with them," Pepper replies. "But maybe we can take pictures with them?"

"Selfies with the pets!" Blythe exclaimed. "Pepper, you're a genius!"

"Well, I don't like to brag, but it is genius, isn't it?" Pepper said with a grin.

"Come to Pawrista's. *Two-for-one treats you'll get, plus a selfie with a pet,*" Zoe rhymed.

"I love it," Blythe said. "I'll make some posters to hang up around town with that rhyme, and maybe some fliers, too!"

Word got around fast about free treats and pet selfies at Pawrista's. Blythe made sure it was okay with all the pets' owners that they could take photos with customers.

The very next day, a local TV reporter showed up at the pet shop to interview Blythe.

"So not only can customers buy one treat or beverage and get one free, they'll be able to take selfies with your pets, is that right, Blythe?" the reporter asked.

"Yes, it is," Blythe said, smiling brightly into the camera. "And we have a great range of pets for customers to choose from—from a gorgeous Cavalier King Charles spaniel to an adorable gecko. It's going to be a great day!"

"It certainly sounds like a terrific idea," the reporter said. "Who wouldn't like to take a picture with one of these cuties?" and the camera panned down to take close-up shots of Penny Ling, Zoe, Sunil, Vinnie, and Minka.

A few of the pets, however, were less than thrilled with this new development.

"Selfies, Blythe. Really?" Russell said in an annoyed voice. "I'm going to have to let strangers pick me up, squeeze me, talk to me, pet me?"

But Sunil was looking forward to it. "Hey, it might be nice," Sunil said.

"And it might be a nightmare," Russell answered. "I'm very particular about who I interact with. I have to say, I'm not happy about this."

"Russell, please," Blythe begged. "You know how important this event is to me. I really need your cooperation."

Eventually, Russell relented. Meanwhile, Pepper was having the opposite reaction.

"What if nobody wants to take a picture with me?" she said. "You know how most people feel about skunks. Talk about awkward!"

"I'm sure there will be people who will want to take a picture with you," Penny Ling said soothingly. "You're being too hard on yourself."

"And if they don't, you're lucky," Russell griped. "I'd trade places with you any day of the week."

"Well, I'm not going to worry about it now," Pepper said. "I think I'm going to get Blythe to give me a little piece of glazed doughnut. Who's with me?"

Penny Ling and Minka weren't hungry.

"I have to keep my girlish figure for my costume," Zoe said.

"Me, too!" Vinnie said, and everyone laughed.

Pepper shrugged. "Okay, more for me!" she said, and bounded out of the room.

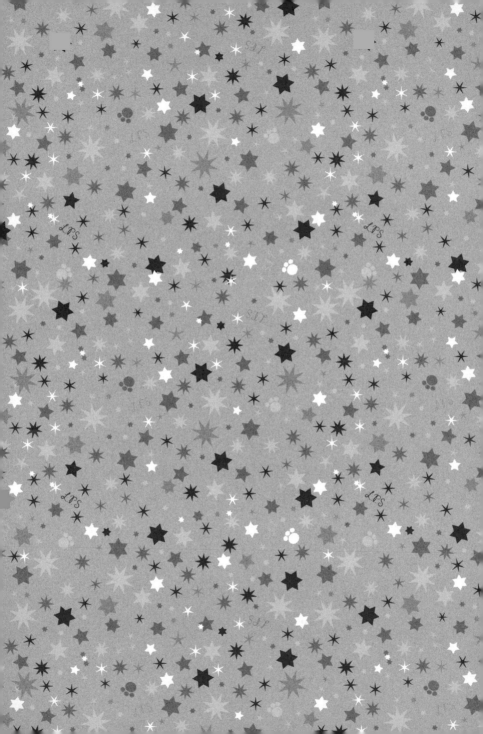

Chapter 8

Pepper's selfie idea turned out to be a great one. Over the next couple of days, nearly every customer who stopped in Pawrista's mentioned the take-a-photo-with-a-pet idea. And the Paris theme was working out beautifully as well. Blythe bought some posters of the Eiffel Tower, the Champs-Élysées, the Seine, and the Louvre to put up the day of

the event. Vinnie and Sunil were still learn-
ing to speak French, slowly but hilariously.
Everyone loved the French outfits Blythe
made for them (especially Zoe). And Blythe
even found some cupcake recipes online
with suggestions for Paris decorations.

"I'm so happy. Everything is perfectly
under control," Blythe said.

"*Ooh*, Blythe, I wish you didn't say that,"
Zoe said.

"Why?" Blythe asked.

"Because it's bad luck. Haven't you
noticed whenever somebody says, 'Everything's fine,' *boom*! Suddenly something
goes wrong?"

"That's ridiculous," Blythe said. "I'm not
going to worry about a silly superstition.
And everything *is* fine."

"Ohhhh." Zoe groaned and put her paws over her eyes. "You're just inviting disaster, Blythe," Zoe said.

Soon things started to unravel.

Zoe kept putting her costume on because she loved it so much, and eventually she tore it. Sunil and Vinnie started bickering over who had the better French accent, Blythe was having a terrible time trying to decorate the cupcakes, and worst of all, Minka wasn't speaking to Pepper.

It all started when Pepper was trying out some new jokes for her comedy routine. "How do you catch a monkey?" she asked Minka. "Climb a tree and act like a banana! What do you call a monkey with a banana in each ear? Anything you want! She can't hear you! *Bwahahaha!*"

At first, Minka laughed, but after a while, Pepper's jokes started to get on her nerves.

"Pepper, maybe you can ease up on the monkey jokes," Minka suggested.

"Why?" Pepper said. "Monkeys are funny. Everyone loves monkey jokes!"

"Except maybe... *monkeys*," Minka said pointedly.

"Oh, Minka, that's ridiculous," Pepper said. "You know I don't mean anything I say. It's just part of my act."

"Well, if it doesn't mean anything to you, then you can just cut it out of your act, can't you?" Minka asked. "Because it means something to me."

"No!" Pepper shouted. "Minka you're just being overly sensitive. I love my monkey jokes, and they are a very important part of my act. The jokes stay."

"And to think *I* was the one who suggested you should perform!" Minka cried. "Well, if those jokes stay, I don't!" Minka stormed out of the room.

Zoe watched as Minka left in a huff and then she looked down at her torn costume.

"Oh, Blythe." She sighed. "I warned you. Why did you ever have to say everything was going well?"

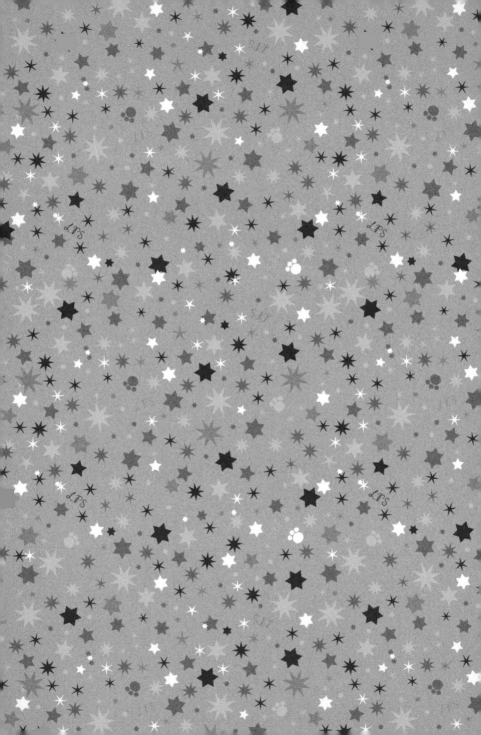

Chapter 9

It was the day before the big event and Blythe was a wreck. Minka and Pepper still weren't speaking, Blythe had to spend an hour fixing Zoe's costume, and decorating the cupcakes was a nightmare. The more Blythe tried to use the gel pen to create designs, the more she turned perfectly good cupcakes into a goopy mess.

"I guess I thought that decorating cupcakes would be easy because I sewed," Blythe said. "I just can't get the hang of this. And I need to have at least six dozen cupcakes decorated with a Paris theme by tomorrow morning. I need help!"

"Poor Blythe!" Penny Ling said. "What are you going to do?"

Blythe took a deep breath and picked up her phone.

"I'm going to call the Biskit twins."

Whittany and Brittany arrived at the Littlest Pet Shop in a flash.

"We're so happy you called us, Blythe," Whittany said. "And Daddy was, too. When we told him he we were going to work he was so happy he started to cry."

"What do you want us to do?" Brittany asked. "And we're not afraid to get our hands dirty. Well…maybe we're a little afraid. I just got a manicure."

"Thanks, guys," Blythe said. She took a deep breath. "Okay, first things first. Please put these on, you don't want to get your clothes dirty." She handed both girls an apron.

"Oh, Brittany, look," Whittany squealed. "We get to wear *costumes*!"

"Not really," Blythe said. "Those aren't costumes. They're just aprons to keep—Oh, never mind. Yeah, you get to wear costumes," Blythe said. "Whatever makes you happy!"

"Hello, how may I help you?" Brittany said to a customer. She turned to Whittany with a big smile. "This is so much fun, Whit. I feel like I'm in a play."

Both girls were surprisingly enthusiastic: They rolled up their sleeves and got to work right away. Russell still eyed them suspiciously. After a little while Whittany spoke up.

"Blythe, how can you stand having all these animals underfoot all the time?" Whittany asked. "I feel like they're all staring at me . . . especially your little porcupine there . . . makes me nervous."

"PORCUPINE!" Russell squealed, tired of being identified as the wrong animal. But of course all Whittany heard was *"Eeee!"*

"I like having my pets around," Blythe said. "And as for them staring at you, why, that's ridiculous. Why would a *hedgehog* be staring at you?"

"I don't know, but he's giving me the willies," Whittany said. Russell glared at her.

"Well, I don't mind having the little doggy around," Brittany said. "She's adorable!"

Zoe, who happened to be wearing a

sparkly purple scarf around her neck, wagged her tail proudly. She turned to the other pets and said, "'If a girl is poorly dressed, you notice her dress, and if she's impeccably dressed, you notice the girl.' Coco Chanel."

Pepper rolled her eyes. "And someone who is annoying will always be annoying, no matter what they're wearing," she said. "Pepper Clark."

Now it was Minka's turn to chime in. "And someone who continues to make fun of their friends, even when one of those friends asks her not to, is *not* a friend. *So there!*"

"*Hmpf!*" Penny Ling agreed, and she and Minka deliberately turned their backs on Pepper and marched away.

Brittany and Whittany watched the fight in amusement.

"That was so funny," Brittany said. "If I didn't know any better—"

"And you *don't*," Russell muttered.

"I'd say that little monkey and panda were mad at the skunk!" Brittany walked over to Pepper. "What did you do, little skunky? Did you make fun of your friends? *Ohh!* I know! Did you spray their favorite outfits?"

"No, but I'll tell you who I'd *like* to spray," Pepper said angrily.

"Pepper, *no!*" Blythe yelled just in the nick of time. She scooped Pepper up in her arms. "Please, not here," she whispered. "Think of your show tomorrow! Think of the cupcakes! If you sprayed in here, everything we've worked so hard for would be over in a flash."

Pepper relented.

"Okay. But I don't like these girls, Blythe," she said.

"I know," Blythe agreed. "Nobody does."

Blythe brought a tray of cupcakes over to Brittany and Whittany as well as a few bowls of different colored frosting and icing gel pens. "We need to decorate these cupcakes," she said. "The theme is Paris, so if there's anything you can think of that would go along with that theme, it would be great."

Whittany picked up a gel pen and drew something on a cupcake. A minute or two later she held up a cupcake to show Blythe. "You mean like this?" she said. Blythe gasped. Whittany had decorated the cupcake with a perfect little Eiffel Tower!

"Or like this?" Brittany asked. She grabbed blue, red, and white gel pens and scribbled on a cupcake. A couple of minutes later she held it up. Now the cupcake was adorned with the French national flag.

"Those are beautiful!" Blythe cried. "How were you able to do that so fast?"

Whittany shrugged. "It's easy. It relaxes me."

Brittany nodded. "It's like . . . you know . . . accessorizing."

They had an entire tray of cupcakes decorated in a flash.

"This is kind of fun," Whittany said. "I mean, not fun like your favorite pair of boots just went on sale, but still, kinda fun, you know, Brit?"

"It is kind of fun," Brittany agreed. "Maybe having one of these job thingies all the time isn't such a bad idea."

"Hey, Blythe, would you hire us full-time?" Whittany asked.

Blythe turned pale. It was one thing to have Whittany and Brittany around for a few hours before a big event, but to have to deal with them every single day would be a totally different story.

"*Kidding!*" Whittany said, and both Biskit twins laughed.

Now that the cupcake-decorating dilemma was over, Pepper saw an opportunity to ask for some more sweets. "Blythe, can I have a little piece of cupcake or doughnut?" she asked sweetly. "You know I'm having a rough morning, especially since Minka isn't speaking to me."

Blythe relented, but not without saying "Pepper, I'm getting a little concerned about your sweet tooth. You have to promise me you're going to try to cut down."

"I will, I will," Pepper promised. Blythe put a little piece of lemon cake on a plate for Pepper. As the tangy sweetness filled her mouth, Pepper smiled to herself. *Why would I ever want to cut down on this? What Blythe doesn't know wouldn't hurt her.* And, while Blythe's back was turned, Pepper quietly knocked a cupcake in an open display case on the floor with her paw and ran off with it.

A little while later, Pepper was chatting with Sunil and Vinnie. She was teasing them about their French accents and clothes. "Whoever heard of a French gecko?" She laughed. "Oh, I can't wait for the customers to get a load of you two in your outfits!" Then she turned to Zoe. "And what about you, Zoe? Are you going to dance the can-can tomorrow?"

Pepper jumped up and started dancing on one of the café tables. *"Bonjour, bonjour!"* she sang out. "Look at me! *Regardez-moi!*

I'm Zoe, the prettiest cancan puppy in the world!" Pepper started dancing crazily.

"Pepper, maybe you should get down from there," Penny Ling said worriedly.

"Why?" Pepper asked. "I feel great! Hey, do you think you could grab another cupcake for me, or maybe a cookie? I could sure use a little more sugar. Or maybe a doughnut? Yeah, that's it! A nice glazed doughnut. Or maybe a slice of pie! *Oooh,* lemon pie! I do love pie! Or cherry!"

"That's *it*!" Russell yelled. "It's time for me to take charge. Pepper, be quiet! And stop dancing on the tabletop. It's dangerous. No more sugar for you. You are out of control."

"I don't know what you're talking about," Pepper replied. "I'm fine. Except…well, now that you mention it, maybe I am a little tired. That dancing wore me out." She jumped down from the table and yawned. "You know what? A little nap right about now sounds like a good idea."

Pepper went off to her bed and slept.

And slept.

And slept.

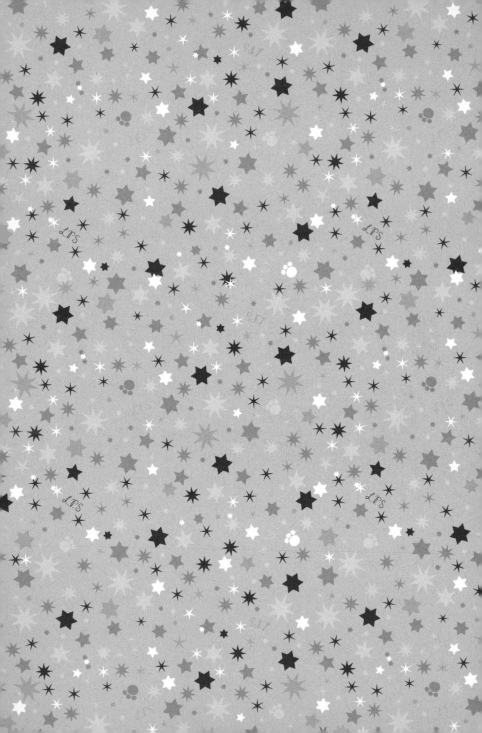

Chapter 10

The day of the big event had finally arrived!

The Pawrista's Café looked beautiful. Blythe strung little twinkling white lights all around the coffee shop and then hung beautiful posters of Paris to add to the mood. All the pets looked terrific in their jaunty French berets and outfits. And Zoe just glowed in her sparkly cancan outfit.

"It looks like you have a wonderful turn-out, Blythe," Mrs. Twombly said. "I'm very proud of you."

The pets peeked out the window. "Look, everybody! There's a line of customers that goes around the block!" Zoe gasped.

"How exciting!" Sunil said.

"You mean *excitant comment*," Vinnie said, saying the same words in French.

The Biskit twins were also there bright and early, much to Blythe's surprise.

"What do you need? What can we do?" they asked Blythe.

"I have to say, I never thought you two would turn out to be such awesome employees," Blythe told them.

"Well, after today, we'll probably never work again in our lives, so we want to make the most of it," Brittany said.

"Let's take a selfie in our work costumes to show Daddy," Whittany said. They both stood behind the counter in their aprons and smiled as Brittany snapped a selfie.

"Well. Whatever your reasons for working here, I'm grateful," Blythe said. "Okay, Mrs. Twombly, open the door!" Blythe said.

Customers rushed in, clutching their two-for-one coupons. The orders came fast and furious.

"Two coffees—one black, one with cream and sugar."

"I'll take a coffee and a blueberry muffin."

"I'll take two cupcakes—give me two with Eiffel Towers—those are cute!"

It was a good thing Whittany and Brittany were there. Even with the three of them behind the counter, they could barely keep up with the demand.

"All these people are here to see us," Whittany said to Brittany proudly.

"Well, not really. They're here to be served by us," Brittany said.

"Either way, we're very important," Whittany said, as a bunch of customers waved their two-for-one coupons in her face. "Who's next?" she yelled.

And where was Pepper? Although Blythe knew people wouldn't be able to understand her comedy routine, she had hoped that Pepper would entertain the other pets while they took selfies with the customers. But Pepper was nowhere to be found.

After the customers had finished their snacks, Whittany and Brittany led them to a separate room to take selfies with the pet of their choice.

Most of the customers who wanted self-ies had children, and the kids squealed with delight when they saw all the pets.

"*Oooh*, look at the pretty doggy!" one lit-tle girl cooed. Whittany handed Zoe to her.

"Now, this kid has got good taste," Zoe said with a big smile. She let the girl cuddle her for a photo.

"I want to take a picture with the hedge-hog," one boy said.

"Well...at least he didn't say porcupine," Russell said, and reluctantly let himself be held for a photograph.

A father with a young son pointed to Vinnie. "Look, Joey, don't you want to hold the lizard?" he asked.

"Okay, Daddy, but I think that's a gecko," the little boy corrected him. Vinnie beamed.

"Smart kid," he whispered.

"What...is...that?" one little girl asked, as she cautiously approached Sunil.

"It's a mongoose," Whittany told her.

"Does he bite?"

"*Hmm*...I don't know...Do you bite?" Whittany asked Sunil.

"*Hmpf!*" Sunil answered. The little girl giggled.

"I don't think Blythe would have a pet here that would bite people," Brittany said. The little girl cautiously put one arm around Sunil and held her camera out with the other for a selfie.

"Okay, smile!" the girl told Sunil, and he happily obliged.

There was a long line for people who wanted to take a photo with Penny Ling. But the longest line was for people who wanted to take their picture with Minka. Minka kept everyone entertained by jumping on customers' shoulders, racing around the room, giving a big cheesy smile for the camera, and basically having loads of fun.

"Monkeys are so funny!" one little boy squealed.

"You see?" Zoe said to Minka. "Everyone thinks monkeys are funny. I don't know why you got so mad at Pepper. I think she was right. I think you overreacted, Minka. I'm sorry, but I'm on Team Pepper in this argument."

All the people waiting to take photos with the pets stared at the dog and monkey chattering to each other.

"It really looks like they're arguing with each other, doesn't it?" one man said with a chuckle.

"Don't be ridiculous," his wife said. "What would animals argue about?"

"Well, I'm on Minka's side," Penny Ling said. "If she was hurting Minka's feelings, she should have stopped making jokes about her."

"But . . . monkeys . . . are . . . actually . . . *funny*!" Zoe protested.

"You don't understand, Zoe," Minka said. "Yes, monkeys may be funny. *I* may be funny. But I'm also a lot of other things, too. I would think Pepper would understand that more than anyone."

"Why?" Zoe said.

"Because most people don't think skunks are anything but stinky," Minka explained. "And I know Pepper is much more than that."

Minka had a point. All the animals were quiet for a moment.

"Okay, the animals have stopped bickering!" the man said. "Now quick, let's take some more pictures while the animals are quiet again!"

One little boy hugged Penny Ling hard as he snapped a photo. But Penny Ling was too busy thinking about what Minka said about Pepper to be upset. And where *was* Pepper anyway?

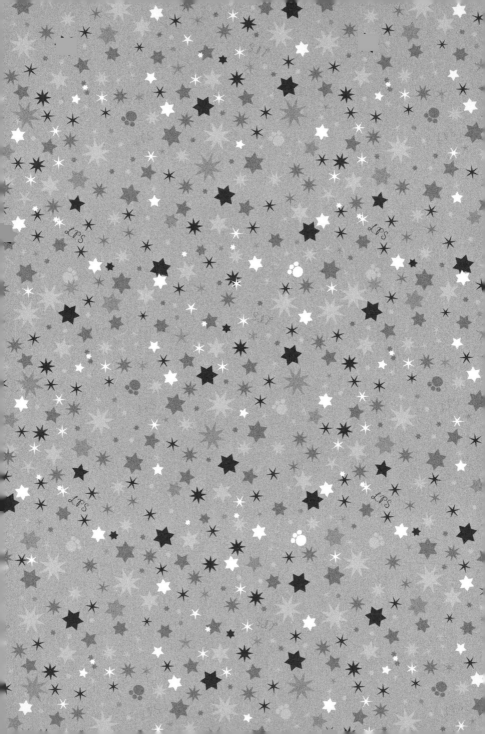

Chapter 11

In the back room, in her bed, Pepper stirred lazily. She knew she had been asleep for quite a while, but she still felt exhausted. And a little bit queasy. She slowly made her way to the front of the pet shop. She blinked. Why were there so many customers? What was going on?

She suddenly remembered everything

in a rush. It was the day of the two-for-one event at Pawrista's! She promised Blythe she was going to perform her comedy act, and instead she slept most of the day away. Pepper felt terrible.

She made her way over to the cash register, where Blythe was counting all the money they'd made so far.

"Blythe," she whispered.

Blythe looked down.

"Oh, Pepper," she gasped. "You look awful. Are you all right?"

"I don't know what's wrong with me," Pepper said. "One minute I felt great. I was talking and laughing and dancing on the countertops. The next thing I know, I'm passed out cold. And now I'm awake, but I still feel tired. And my stomach feels all rumbly."

"I know exactly what's wrong with you," Russell said. "You were on a sugar high and you crashed."

"Pepper, *now* do you understand why I was trying to limit your sweets?" Blythe said. "Too much sugar is a dangerous thing. It makes you feel good for a little while, but then you come crashing down. It's awful."

"You're telling me," Pepper groaned. "I can't remember the last time I felt this bad. But most of all, I'm sorry I let you down, Blythe."

"Oh, don't worry," Blythe assured her. "The event is going well. The only problem is—"

"Excuse me, miss," a customer said. "Can you recommend a strong coffee?"

"*That's* the problem," Blythe said to Pepper.

People keep asking me about coffee. I don't know anything about coffee."

"A good strong coffee is Kona dark," Pepper told her.

Blythe was shocked. "How do you know about coffee?" she asked.

"I don't drink it, but like I told you, Blythe, I love the way it smells," Pepper said. "I can tell you all about different kinds of coffee by what they smell like."

Just then another customer came over.

"I'd like a smooth, rich coffee," he said.

Blythe looked at Pepper.

"French roast," Pepper said.

"The last time I was here I had a coffee that had a slightly sweet, nutty taste," a woman said to Blythe. "I can't remember what kind it was. Can you help me?"

Again, Blythe looked at Pepper for help.

"Hazelnut," Pepper told Blythe.

It turned out Pepper really knew all about coffee! She was able to pick the perfect coffee for each customer just by its scent. And she saved the day for Blythe.

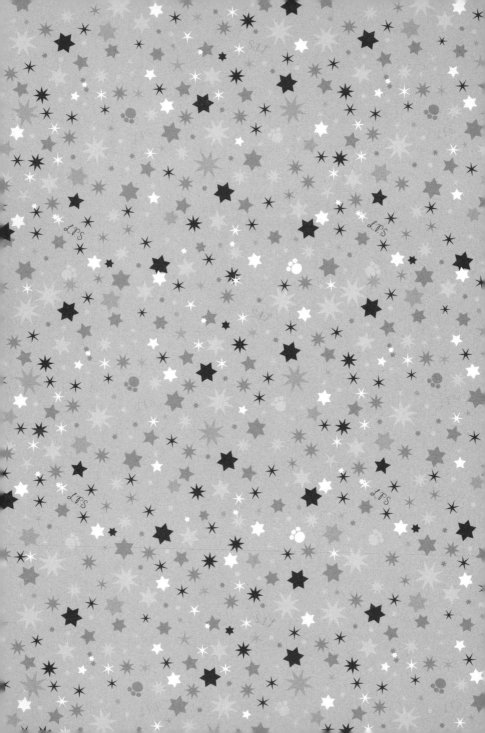

Chapter 12

Sunil and Vinnie were both in a bad mood. They were disappointed.

"What a huge waste of time those French lessons were," Vinnie said. "There isn't anybody here who looks the least bit French."

"I guess it was silly of us to think that because the event had a French theme, someone who actually was French would show up," Sunil said. It looked like there wasn't anybody there for them to speak French to. Until…

A young woman came in with a beautiful French poodle. The dog was wearing a little yellow bow in her hair and matching boots. Zoe loved her outfit.

"Look at that poodle," Zoe whispered to Penny Ling. "Now that's what I call style!"

"Bonjour," Sunil said to the pretty little poodle. *"Tu es très jolie."*

Vinnie took a quick peek in his French book. *"Vous êtes très belle en jaune,"* he said. *You're very beautiful in yellow.*

The poodle wagged her tail and wriggled in delight. She began speaking very quickly in French. *"Vous parlez français tous les deux! Comme c'est merveilleux!"* She said, "You both speak French! How wonderful!"

but of course Sunil and Vinnie didn't know that. They both frantically looked in their French books.

"Um ... *oui*," Sunil said.

"Ditto," Vinnie said.

The poodle laughed. "Ah! So you only speak a *leetle* French. That is okay. I speak a *leetle* English. I am Fifi, and pleased to meet you both."

Sunil and Vinnie both raced to her side in a flash!

"Fifi, would you like to take a picture with an all-American gecko?" Vinnie asked.

"But of course!" Fifi said with a smile.

"Blythe!" Vinnie hissed. "Take our picture!" He quickly put his arm around Fifi.

"Adorable!" Blythe said. "Say *fromage*!"

"You mean *cheese*!" Vinnie said.

"That's what I said," Blythe assured him.

Not to be outdone, Sunil rushed to Fifi's side with a little plate of pastries. "Some sweets for my sweet?" he said.

Fifi's owner laughed. "Why, Fifi, I do believe that a mongoose and a gecko both have crushes on you," he said.

Meanwhile, Vinnie was annoyed with Sunil. "I saw her first," he said.

"But my French is better!" Sunil replied.

Fifi laughed. "There is no need to fight," she said. "We can all be friends, *oui?*"

"Fine," Sunil grumbled. "But I still say my French is better!"

When there was a brief lull in the front of the coffee shop, Pepper decided to join the rest of the pets in the back room for selfies.

The minute Penny Ling saw her, she broke out in a big grin.

"Pepper's here!"

All the pets smiled, except for Minka. She was still mad.

"Minka, can't you just forgive and forget?" Penny Ling asked. "I'm sure Pepper is sorry."

Minka tossed her head. "If she's sorry she hasn't said anything to me about it. She has to apologize."

Suddenly, one of the women noticed Pepper and let out a bloodcurdling scream.

"*Skunk!*" she yelled. "There's a *skunk* in here!"

And just like that—it turned from a peaceful afternoon to absolute bedlam.

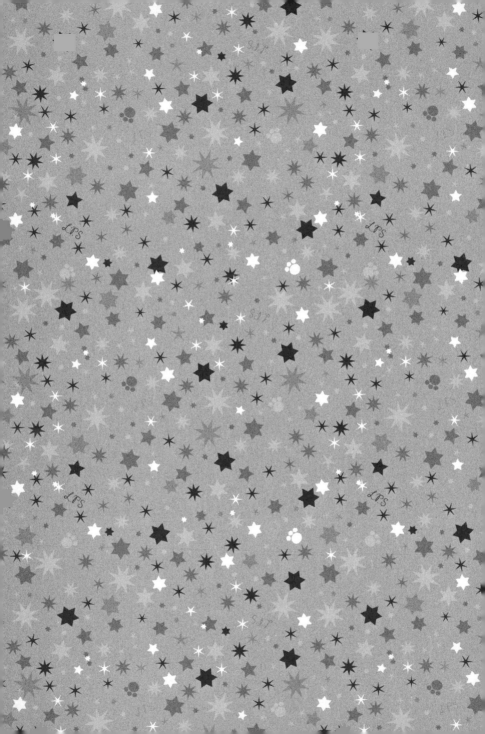

Chapter 13

Adults and children started racing out of the selfie room as fast as they could. Some even demanded their money back. All the people who had been smiling and happy just a few minutes before now were furious.

"You didn't say you had a skunk on the premises!"

"It could spray us at any moment! Get me out of here!"

"I'm going to call the board of health!" someone shouted.

"I'm going to sue!" shouted another.

Blythe was bewildered. People were running in all directions, yelling and screaming.

"What's going on?" she asked.

"It's the skunk," Whittany said. "Nobody wants to be in the same room with a skunk."

"And I can't say that I blame them," said Brittany loudly.

Pepper felt terrible. Blythe's event was ruined and it was all her fault. But what made it worse was it wasn't because she was eating too much sugar, or dancing on the tabletop, or yelling and screaming, or even sleeping. It was just because she existed. Why did people hate skunks so much?

All the pets felt terrible for Pepper—even Minka. They realized they had to do something to save the event from being a total disaster.

Penny Ling grabbed some ribbons from the Paris decorations and quickly started an impromptu ribbon dance. Sunil snatched some doughnuts off a plate and began juggling them. A few children stopped running and pointed. Then a few more spoke.

"Look, Mommy, the panda is dancing!"

"Hey, is that mongoose doing a juggling act? Let's wait a minute and watch this."

Zoe started singing. Of course, to the customers it just sounded like a dog yipping, but she looked so cute in her costume, nobody seemed to care.

All the pets tried their best to entertain the customers. They wanted them to forget about being afraid that a skunk had been in their midst. They wanted people to stay, to enjoy themselves, to continue taking selfies and having a good time.

Their plan worked! Within a few minutes, everyone had forgotten about Pepper (who quietly slipped away while the customers were yelling).

As Pepper heard the customers talking and laughing about the other pets in the selfie room, she couldn't stop feeling bad about herself. People hated her—without even knowing her. It just didn't seem fair.

Suddenly, Pepper heard a familiar voice.

"Where is she? Where is the most beautiful skunk in the world?"

Pepper peeked back into the selfie room.

It was Benny! Benny was a tomcat who had mistaken Pepper for a cat for a little while. But even after he realized she was a skunk, they still remained good friends. Benny was there with his owner, Sarah, who was holding him.

Sarah spotted Pepper peeking around the corner. "Oh, look, Benny, there's your friend!" she said. She put Benny down on the floor. "Go say hello."

Sarah turned to the other customers who were upset about Pepper. "I really don't know what all the fuss is about," she told them. "Don't you people realize skunks only spray as a last measure of protection to defend themselves? If you leave them alone, they won't spray. And especially not Pepper! Why, she's the dearest little skunk I've ever met. My little tomcat, Benny, here is quite taken with her. They are very good friends."

The customers couldn't believe it.

"Your cat is friends with a skunk?"

Sarah nodded. She then pointed to Benny and Pepper. "If you don't believe me, just see for yourself," she said.

The stunned customers stared in shock as Benny and Pepper cuddled like best friends.

"Let's go in the back room where we can talk," Pepper said.

"How are you, my love?" Benny asked. "You're looking well."

"I'm okay, Benny," Pepper told him. "It's been a rough day, though. The customers don't want me around, and Minka and I are not speaking."

"Why not?" Benny asked. "You and Minka have always been such good friends."

"It all started with my comedy act," Pepper said. "I made a few jokes about monkeys, and they bothered Minka. She asked me to take them out, but I refused."

"Why?" Benny asked.

"They were only harmless jokes, Benny," Pepper said. "Everybody knows monkeys are funny! Minka was being overly sensitive. Why? Do you think I was wrong?"

Benny considered this.

"You know, my love, I think the world of you. But in this case I think you are being unfair to your friend Minka. Maybe monkeys are funny, but isn't your friend Minka much more than just a funny monkey? You are acting like the people who don't want to meet you because you are a skunk. Aren't you much more than a skunk?"

Pepper realized Benny was right. "I have to apologize to Minka right away!" But would her friend forgive her?

Pepper went into the selfie room and marched right over to Minka. "Minka, I am so sorry," she said. "I was being selfish and just thinking of myself. Can you ever forgive me?"

Minka immediately threw her arms around Pepper. "Of course I forgive you!" she said. "And I was the one who was wrong. I was just being overly sensitive. After all, monkeys *are* funny."

"But you are so much more than a just funny monkey," Pepper said. "You're talented, and sweet, and beautiful, and creative, and most important of all, you are a wonderful friend."

"And you are so much more than a skunk," Minka said. "You're funny, and witty, and smart, and most important of all, you're a wonderful friend too…and you're *my* friend."

"*Ahhh*, I love happy endings!" Benny said.

All the pets cheered.

"Thank goodness everyone is friends again," Blythe said. "I was worried about how things were going to work around here if two of my pets weren't speaking to each other."

"Oh, Blythe, you should have known we couldn't stay mad at each other for long," Pepper said. "Although I have to admit, I was getting a little worried myself."

"Hey, Blythe, look…" Whittany said. "Your little skunk and monkey are going to be famous."

Blythe looked around. All the customers

were snapping photos of Pepper and Minka hugging!

Everyone was sending photos of Pepper and Minka to their friends.

"Why, Minka, I do believe we're going viral!" Pepper laughed.

"This is the cutest thing I've ever seen," one man said.

"I'm going to make this my wallpaper," another woman said.

Within ten minutes, the Littlest Pet Shop and Pawrista's Café were more crowded than ever. People were coming from all over just to see the adorable monkey and skunk hugging!

"Blythe, look! We've completely sold out all our cupcakes and cookies," Mrs. Twombly cried. Nobody cared. They just wanted to take selfies with the pets.

Blythe looked up and was surprised to see Kat from Kat's Coffee Shop waiting to take a selfie. Kat laughed when she saw the shocked look on Blythe's face.

"I closed up my coffee shop for the day about ten minutes ago," she said. "As soon as someone sent me a photo of your pets hugging, I knew I couldn't compete with that! Plus, I wanted to see it for myself."

Zoe turned to Russell. "You know what? We should all start hugging," she said.

"What?" Russell said. "C'mon, Zoe, you know I'm not a touchy-feely kind of guy."

"Oh, get over it, Russell," Zoe said. "Don't you realize if we all start hugging, these people will love it? Do it for Blythe. And besides, you know I hate it when I'm not the center of attention. So ... *hug me!*" she commanded.

Russell did what he was told.

"Okay! Now Penny Ling, hug Sunil. And then hug Vinnie," Zoe ordered. "And then someone else trade places with Russell and come hug me!"

Zoe was right. The customers couldn't get over the lovefest at the pet shop. They all lined up for a fresh round of selfies, and this time the longest line was for Pepper— the skunk who started it all!

"I always said skunks were actually adorable creatures," one woman said.

Pepper couldn't believe it. It was the same woman who screamed "Skunk!" and started all the chaos. Pepper rolled her eyes, but Minka nudged her.

"Just go with it," Minka advised. "It's better than having people hate you for no reason, right? If that woman wants to make believe she always liked you, just go with it."

"All right, all right," Pepper mumbled. "I'll put up with it for *you*, Minka!"

The same TV reporter who had visited the pet shop a few days before the event walked over to Blythe. "This is such a feel-good story, it's going to be the lead piece on the news tonight," he told her. I'm going to start it off by saying, "We can all take a lesson from the pets at the Littlest Pet Shop. Why can't we all just get along?"

Blythe laughed. "Well, you know, the pets are just like people," she said. "They argue, they fight, but happily, they always do make up and become friends again."

Mrs. Twombly heard Blythe and laughed. "Oh, Blythe, you have such a wonderful imagination," she said. She turned to the reporter. "She actually thinks the pets talk to each other and fight like people! Have you ever heard of such a thing?"

Russell smiled to himself. *Mrs. Twombly, you have no idea,* he thought.

Blythe had an idea.

"Attention, everyone!" she said. The room was instantly quiet.

"You all now know how loving and affectionate my pets are," she said. "But did you know they are also talented? Pepper Clark, the skunk you were all so afraid of, is actually a very talented comedienne."

"Blythe . . . ?" Pepper whispered.

"And I'm sure if you all put your hands together and give her a round of applause, she would love to perform."

The applause was deafening.

Blythe knew that to humans Pepper's comedy routine would sound only like an animal squeaking, but she also knew they would stick around to hear it. Pepper would be performing to a full house. It would be her dream come true!

Pepper walked to the front of the selfie room. Russell grabbed the flashlight and shined it on Pepper like a spotlight. Pepper began her routine. And she talked only about coffee and treats, and left out any mention of animals in her act.

"Hello, friends! Ever notice that when you serve someone a cold cup of coffee, it makes them boiling mad? Does your coffee taste like dirt? It should—it was just ground a couple of minutes ago! A man went to a doctor and said, 'Every time I drink coffee I get a stabbing pain in my eye.' The doctor said, 'Maybe you should try taking the spoon out first!'"

All the pets howled and cheered, and the customers loved it.

One woman nudged her husband. "Look, honey, our poodle is actually listening to the skunk. It's like the skunk is really telling jokes!"

"I would never have believed it unless I saw it with my own eyes," another customer said in astonishment.

"Pepper, you're a hit! Everyone loves you!" Minka cheered.

Pepper smiled and bowed as the crowd applauded.

Suddenly, one customer sniffed the air appreciatively. "*Mmm*, what's that heavenly smell?" he asked.

It was Pepper! Pepper was so happy when she performed she let out a scent just like her favorite coffee drink—and the whole café smelled like mocha spice latte.

One customer stopped to speak to Blythe as she was leaving the pet shop. "Hang on to that skunk, dear, she's a treasure!" she said.

"Oh, I will," Blythe replied. She smiled as she saw a line forming halfway around the block. Everyone wanted to take a selfie with Pepper Clark—superstar!

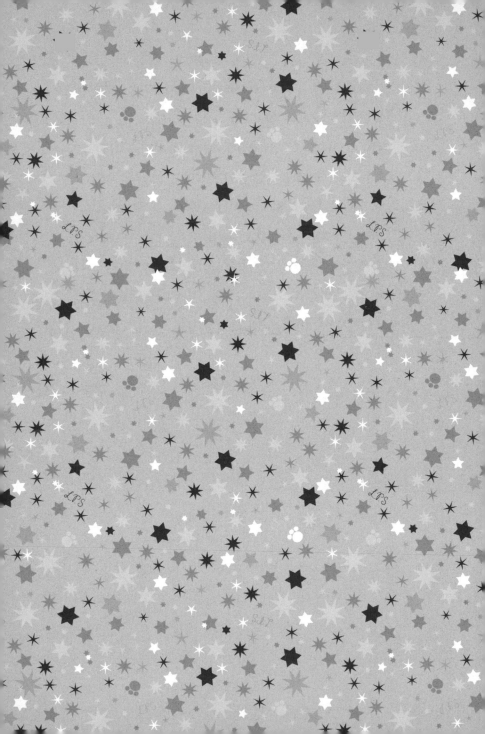

Turn the page for a look at

AVAILABLE NOW!

Chapter 1

"Minka, stop fidgeting," Blythe said to the cute pink spider monkey. "The Pet Pageant is only two weeks away, and I need to finish your outfit, plus all the other pets'."

Minka grinned. "I know, Blythe! But I'm just so excited about the pageant! And I love my new outfit!" Minka suddenly jumped away from Blythe to look at herself in a full-length mirror. "Ouch!" Minka yelped as she jumped.

"I told you to stop fidgeting," Blythe said again. "I was pinning the hem on your skirt when you jumped."

The two stood in front of the mirror together. "Oh, Blythe, it's just beautiful," Minka gasped.

"It did turn out pretty nice, if I do say so myself," Blythe agreed. Blythe's creation was a sky-blue sundress with straps that crisscrossed in the back.

Minka gave Blythe a hug. "You're the best designer in the whole world!" she cried.

Blythe laughed as she hugged Minka back. "And you're the sweetest spider monkey," she replied.

Ring-a-ling!

Everyone in the pet store turned to see who was at the door. It was Lewis, the neighborhood letter carrier, with a package for Blythe. He looked at Minka and Blythe hugging and smiled. "I've always read that monkeys are very affectionate creatures," he said. "I guess it's true."

"Oh, it's true all right," Blythe answered, with a quick glance at Minka to keep quiet. Blythe had a big secret—she could communicate with animals. And she wanted to make sure that her secret stayed a secret. While other people just heard barks, squawks, growls, chirps, and meows, Blythe heard actual words. She realized this talent was a great gift, and she didn't want to share it with the world. She was able to help the animals when they needed her, and they were able to help her, too. At first, Blythe found her ability a little scary, but now she wouldn't change things for the world.

Blythe looked down at the package Lewis handed her. "Oh, this must be the special fabric I ordered for the Pet Pageant," she said. "Thank you so much, Lewis!"

Just at that moment, Zoe came running over. "Did I hear you say 'special fabric'?" she asked. The Cavalier King Charles spaniel started pawing the package curiously.

Lewis couldn't hear what she said, of course. All he heard was a dog yipping excitedly and pawing at the package. "Well! Isn't she a nosy little thing?" Lewis said with a grin. "You'd almost think she knew what was in that package!"

"Almost," Blythe agreed. She waited until Lewis was gone to open the package.

Zoe sighed happily as she gazed at the bolts of soft silk and shiny satin. "Oh, I can't wait to see what you're going to use this for," she said.

"Don't worry, Zoe," Blythe assured her. "Even though you can't enter the Pet Pageant this year, I'm going to make you a new outfit, too."

Zoe gave a little pout. "Tell me again— why can't I enter this year?"

"Because you won last year," Blythe reminded her. "And were first runner-up the year before that. The judges decided it just wasn't fair to the other pets participating. You need to give some other pets a chance, Zoe," she said gently.

"I guess I can understand that," Zoe said with a sigh as she admired her reflection in a mirror.

Blythe laughed at Zoe looking at herself. "The Perfect Pet Pageant isn't all about beauty. The judges also consider the joy the pets bring to their owners, and their unique talents."

Zoe looked around at the pets in the pet shop. "We certainly have a lot of possible winners here," she said. "Since I can't compete this time, maybe I'll help mentor some of the pets. You know, give them tips on poise, beauty, and talent."

"That would be awesome," Blythe told her. "You're the most poised and glamorous pet I know!"

"Me too!" Zoe agreed. She looked around the pet shop, her eyes sparkling with excitement. "I can't wait to turn these pets into pageant stars!"

Littlest Pet Shop
Mysteries At The Pet Shop

NOW ON DVD!